WHITNEY RIDES THE WHALE WITH JONAH

and learns she can't run away

THE EMERALD BIBLE ☆ ☆ ☆ COLLECTION

THERESE JOHNSON BORCHARD

ILLUSTRATIONS BY WENDY VANNEST

Therese J. Borchard

PAULIST PRESS
NEW YORK / MAHWAH, N.J.

ISBN: 0–8091–6663–1

Published by Paulist Press
997 Macarthur Boulevard
Mahwah, New Jersey 07430

Printed and bound in the United States of America

The Emerald Bible Collection
is dedicated
to the loving memory of
Whitney Bickham Johnson

TABLE OF CONTENTS

NANA'S EMERALD BIBLE

It was a warm August morning the day the Bickham family moved from their Michigan home to a residence in a western suburb of Chicago. Mr. Bickham's mother, Nana, who had lived with the family for some time, had passed away in February of that same year. Not long after, Mr. Bickham landed a great new job; however, it meant the whole family would have to leave everything that was familiar to them in Michigan and start again in Chicago.

It was especially hard on Whitney and Howard, the two Bickham children. They had grown accustomed to their school in Michigan and had several friends there. They didn't want to have to start over at a new school. Whitney, especially, was heartbroken about moving away from Michigan, for Nana's death alone had been very difficult on her. For Whitney, the Bickhams' Michigan home was filled with wonderful memories of Nana that she did not want to leave behind.

Nana and Whitney had had a very special friendship. Since Mrs. Bickham worked a day job that kept her very busy, it was Nana that had cared for Whitney from the time she was a baby. Growing up, Whitney spent endless hours with Nana. Her most wonderful memories of Nana centered around those afternoons when the two would go down to the basement and read stories from the Bible. Nana would sit on her favorite chair and read a story to

Whitney that related in some way to a problem Whitney was having. As Whitney sat on her grandma's lap listening to the story, her own situation always became a little clearer.

When Nana became sick and knew she was going to die, she called Whitney into her room and said:

"Dear Whitney, you know how special you are to me. I want you to have something that will always bring you home to me. I have a favorite possession that I'd like to leave with you—my Emerald Bible. Every time you open this special book, you will find yourself in another world—at a place far away from your own, and in a time way before your birth. But I will be right there with you."

Nana was so weak that she could barely go on, but, knowing the importance of her message, she pushed herself to say these last words:

"Whatever you do in the years

ahead, keep this Bible with you, as it
will help you with all of life's most
difficult lessons. And remember, when
you open its pages, I am there with
you."

As Nana closed her eyes to enter
into an eternal sleep,
Whitney spotted the
beautiful Emerald Bible
that lay at Nana's side. It
sparkled like a massive
jewel, and on its cover
were engraved the words,
"Lessons of Life."

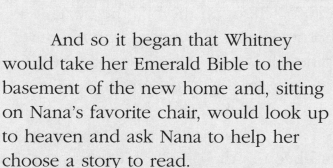

And so it began that Whitney
would take her Emerald Bible to the
basement of the new home and, sitting
on Nana's favorite chair, would look up
to heaven and ask Nana to help her
choose a story to read.

CHAPTER ONE

THE NIGHT BEFORE SCHOOL

It was the evening before Whitney's first day of fifth grade at her new school. She was so nervous thinking about the next day that she gave herself a bad stomachache. Just imagining the ride to school on the bus the next morning sent chills up and down her spine. She couldn't believe that she wasn't going back to her old, familiar school in Michigan.

For two months now, the family had been in their new Chicago home, and Whitney had not made a single new friend. Sure, there were other kids in the neighborhood that would get together

THE EMERALD BIBLE COLLECTION

and play kickball in the street, but she hadn't found anyone like Molly or Sue back at home. The three of them used to spend hours together on summer afternoons. They'd bake cookies and make lemonade and go on long bike rides. Rainy days were especially fun because Nana would read them stories and tell them old tales.

But now Whitney was lonely. Molly and Sue were not around to laugh and play with, and Nana had died. Gone were the days when Whitney could close her eyes and listen for hours and hours to one of Nana's stories.

"If only I could go back to my old basement in Michigan and sit on Nana's lap!" Whitney thought to herself. "If only

13

I could go back to Nana's world of imagination and wonder."

Whitney's mom, Mrs. Bickham, knew how special Nana was to Whitney. Although Whitney and her mom were very close, Mrs. Bickham realized that she could never fill that spot in Whitney's heart that was missing Nana. Mrs. Bickham and Whitney would often talk about what had happened at school or with Whitney's friends, but seldom did Whitney confide in her mom as she did with Nana. Whitney saved her special problems and concerns for Nana, because she knew that Nana would always read her a story that would make her feel much better.

"Just this once, I wish I knew what Nana would say to Whitney," Mrs. Bickham said to Mr. Bickham as the two prepared for bed. "I know that I cannot replace Nana, but I just wish I could say something to make little Whitney feel better," she continued to explain to her husband.

Whitney's mom and dad were both worried about Whitney. They were sad that Nana couldn't be with Whitney to read her a story before her big day. They each had tried to comfort Whitney in their own ways. Earlier in the day, Mr. Bickham had taken Whitney for a car ride around some nearby neighborhoods. Mrs. Bickham had baked a batch of Whitney's favorite sugar cookies. But neither attempt lifted their daughter's spirits.

"I will try one last time to calm her," Mrs. Bickham said to Mr. Bickham as she pulled her nightshirt over her head. "I cannot read stories to my dear Whitney in the same way Nana did, but maybe I can say something to put her at ease."

Mrs. Bickham walked down the long hallway to Whitney's room and 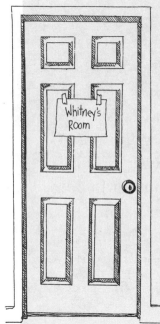 knocked several times on her bedroom door. She paused for a while and knocked again. But there was no answer.

"Where in the world could she have wandered to at this time of night?" Mrs. Bickham asked herself, praying that Whitney didn't do anything drastic, like run away from home.

"Ah, the basement," she said under her breath. "I bet she wanted to have a quiet moment with Nana, even if Nana cannot be physically there. Some time on Nana's favorite chair might make her feel better. I will let her be."

16

Sure enough, Whitney was in the basement, seated on Nana's favorite chair, with her dog, Bailey, on her lap. The sad ten-year-old sat on the comfortable chair, sobbing, burying her wet, teary face into her hands. Between sniffles, she talked to her furry friend, who was now her best buddy since Nana was gone.

"What would Nana say to me tonight?" Whitney asked Bailey. "What story would she read to me?"

Whitney knew that her pup would not be able to utter the wise words that Nana always had, but his being at her side helped her talk about her fears.

"I can't go to that stupid new school tomorrow. I don't know anyone. Who will I sit with at lunch? Who will play with me at recess?"

As Whitney imagined her next day at school, new tears formed in her eyes and rolled down her cheeks. She had cried so much by now that she didn't care about how damp her face had become. She was too tired to catch the tears. Exhausted, she let the wet drops roll off the side of her face, into Bailey's fur coat.

As she grimaced, a serious expression came over Whitney's face. It appeared as if she was thinking long and hard about something. Indeed, she was. She was trying to come up with a scheme for the following morning, a plan that would allow her to avoid the first day of school.

There was silence. And then a guilty smirk. Periodically Whitney would squint her eyes, thinking hard about exactly how the plan would work. Her eyes shifted focus, moving from one side to the other, looking up and then down and then up again. After about ten minutes of intense thinking, she was completely frustrated and continued her conversation with Bailey.

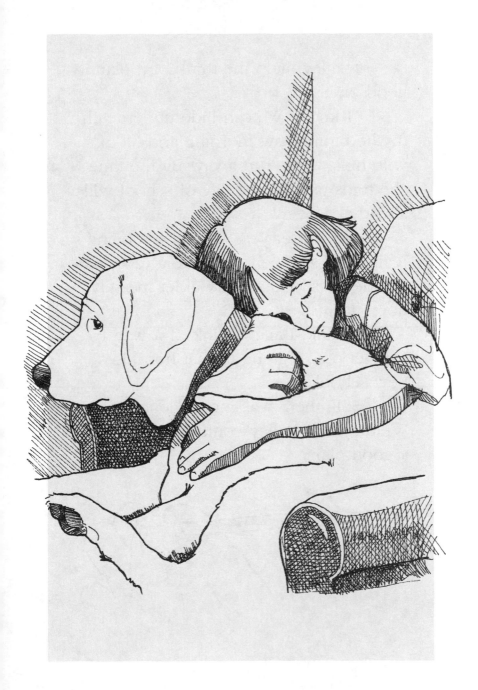

"Bailey, help me think of a plan. A good one.

"I know! We can hide underneath my bed tomorrow morning and Mom will think we've run away! By the time she finds us, the first day of school will already be over.

"Or, better yet! What about being really sick? Maybe I can fake a fever of 102 degrees, and Mom will let me stay home to rest.

"Think, Bailey, think of a way I can get out of going to that horrible new school."

Still, there was more silence. Whitney and Bailey could not think up a good plan.

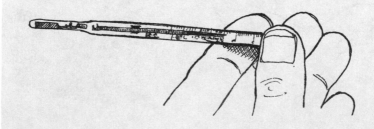

Then Whitney remembered the Emerald Bible that Nana left her. She thought about the words Nana spoke to her just before dying: "Whatever you do in the years ahead, keep this Bible with you, as it will help you with all of life's most difficult lessons. And remember, when you open its pages, I am there with you."

Because the Bickham family had not completely unpacked from their move, many items were still boxed up in the basement. Among these things was the Emerald Bible. Afraid that it might get lost in the shuffle, Mrs. Bickham made sure to pack the Bible securely with other precious things, like the family's photo albums.

Whitney went over to the dozens of boxes that were stored in the corner of the basement. She searched through three boxes, but had no luck finding her Bible. As she started to pull apart the fourth box, she noticed something green sparkling from behind the other items. Tucked away in a dusty box with other things from the move 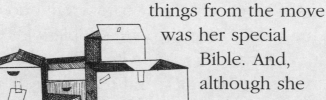 was her special Bible. And, although she had not touched it for months, its cover still shone as bright as the day it lay beside Nana, radiating everything around it.

The time had come for Whitney to use this precious gift that Nana had left her. A little nervous, Whitney rested the Emerald Bible on her lap, next to Bailey. Looking up to heaven, she said, "Nana, read me a story tonight. Choose a story of wisdom for me."

Rays of light emerged from the Bible as Whitney gently opened the Emerald cover. This indeed was a special book. Its chapters were beautifully stitched together with golden thread, and the texture of its pages was soft, like cloth. Tenderly, she thumbed through the delicate sheets until her eyes stopped at a certain paragraph. She began to read aloud . . .

"There once lived a man named Jonah, who disobeyed the Lord and tried to run away from him. God had ordered Jonah to go to the city of Nineveh and tell the people there that because of their sinful ways the city would soon be destroyed. Jonah was afraid to do this, and so, in an attempt to escape from God, Jonah boarded a sailors' ship and sailed with them away from his land."

CHAPTER TWO

ALL ABOARD!

As soon as Whitney looked up from reading the paragraph, she found herself not on Nana's chair in the basement of her Chicago home, but seated on the deck of a large ship in the middle of the sea. She was relieved to see that she was still holding Bailey in one arm, and her Emerald Bible in the other.

"Where the heck are we?" Whitney turned to Bailey and asked.

"You're on my ship, that's where," an angry sailor replied to her question.

"But how did we get here?" Whitney continued.

"That's what I'd like to know," the sailor said, gawking at her as if she was some kind of alien. "This is no place for a young girl like yourself."

"Can you at least tell me where we are?" Whitney politely requested. She was beginning to feel frightened.

"The eastern side of the Great Sea, a couple of miles off the coast. You know where that is?"

"I'm afraid I don't," Whitney honestly answered. "How far are we from Chicago?"

"From where? I haven't heard of that place."

With a look of confusion and fear, Whitney hugged Bailey close to her and whispered in his ear, "I'm afraid we're lost, Bailey."

Just then, fierce winds began to rock the ship. Everything that was aboard began to slide from one side of the boat to the other. The people on the deck became very dizzy and, holding on to anything stable or secure in sight, they began to panic.

"Is the ship going to sink? What is going to happen to us? What should we do?" they all began to scream and shout.

Even the captain looked alarmed. Wanting to know exactly who was on his ship, he said to one of his men, "Gather all of the passengers on the deck."

The sailor then went down below the deck to the hold of the ship to see if anyone had sought shelter there. He searched each compartment and found no one. Then, as soon as he was ready to make his way up the stairs, he spotted a man sleeping in between two very large boxes. The man, whose name was Jonah—meaning "dove of faithfulness or truthfulness"—was hiding in the place where the crew kept their cargo.

"Wake up!" the shipman yelled at Jonah. "This boat is about to break in half, and you are sleeping soundly here? Call on your God. Help us!"

The man dragged Jonah up the stairs with him and told the captain about Jonah's hiding between the boxes.

"Are you the reason for this disaster?" the captain asked Jonah. "Before we set out, the skies were clear; we had perfect conditions for sailing. But soon after we left the coast, storm clouds came over us from out of nowhere. It seems as if the gods are angry!"

"Tell us, Jonah, who is your god? And might he be enraged for some reason?" the team of sailors on the deck questioned him.

"My God is the God of Israel, the one Lord of the heaven and the earth," Jonah explained. At hearing this, the crewmen became even more afraid that this powerful God whom Jonah described was punishing all of the people aboard the ship for something Jonah had done.

"And tell us, what are you doing hiding on our ship?" the sailors continued with their interrogation. "Are you trying to flee this God of yours?"

"Well . . . ," Jonah hesitated.

"Well . . . yes," he finally admitted to them.

"And what shall we do to you so that the waters quiet down for us?" the men asked. "Surely we cannot throw you into the sea and leave you to die. But your being on our ship puts all of us who are aboard in danger."

Jonah and the men paused, thinking about their options. Whitney and Bailey, still confused about where they were, just listened and observed the conversation from afar. They were afraid to interject any comments to this rough group of seamen.

"Let us try to bring the ship back to land," suggested one of the crew. "If we can at least get in sight of the coast we will be safer."

The others agreed, and so the team of sailors turned the boat around and started back the way they came. But the winds only grew fiercer, and the water wilder.

Finally, Jonah spoke up, knowing that the only real solution was to get him off of the ship.

"Throw me off board, men. I am causing the violent storms. With me on this ship, the conditions will only grow worse."

The men knew Jonah was speaking the truth, but they were afraid that his God would seek revenge with them if they threw him into the sea to die. So they decided to pray to the God of Israel, asking for his mercy and compassion.

"Lord of the heaven and of the earth, do not punish us for what we are about to do," they prayed. "For we do it so to please you."

And with these words, the sailors picked up Jonah and threw him into the turbulent sea.

Immediately the storm ceased, and the waters quieted. The winds calmed so that the ship no longer rocked from one side to the other.

However, Whitney and Bailey, still watching all of the activity from across the deck, panicked when they saw that Jonah was tossed into the sea. Without hesitation, Whitney burst out, "Hurry, Bailey, we have to save him!"

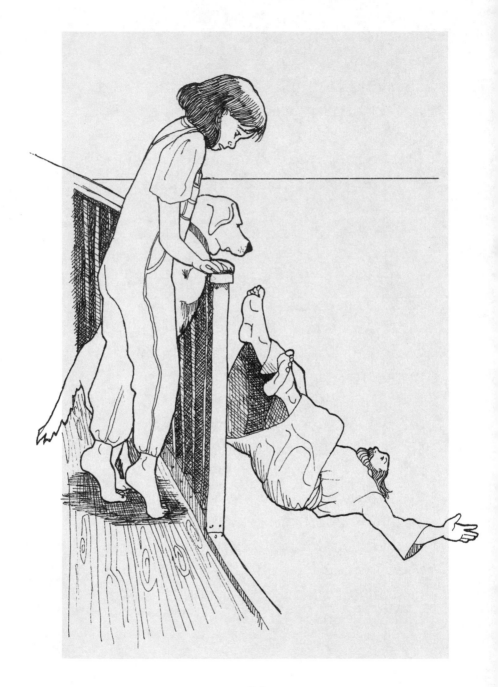

34

Whitney was an excellent swimmer, and she loved the water. She was confident as she dove into the sea that she and Bailey would be fine. However, as the first cold rush of current caught her, she gasped for air, trying her best to hang on to Bailey with one hand and her Bible with the other.

CHAPTER THREE

THE BIG FISH

W hitney, Bailey, and Jonah were now all trying to stay afloat in the sea, bobbing around in the moving water like buoys marking a channel. The temperature was numbing, and so all three looked for logs and other items in the sea that they might climb atop of.

But God was with Jonah, Whitney, and Bailey, and provided more than a large log or debris to hang onto. Not even five minutes after Whitney had plunged into the water did an enormous fish swim near the three and swallow up all of them whole, so as to not injure any of them.

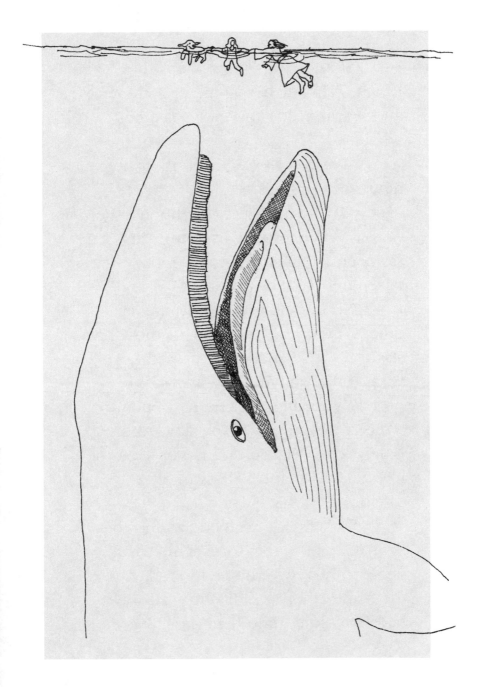

Strangely enough, there they were: Jonah, Whitney, and Bailey, comfortable and warm inside the belly of a big whale.

Whitney looked around at her new surroundings.

"This whale must be huge!" she said to whoever was listening. "Its stomach is bigger than my entire basement back in Chicago!"

No one responded. Jonah sat quietly in a remote corner of the whale's stomach. It seemed as if he did not want to be bothered by anyone, probably feeling as if he had been harassed enough for one day. And Bailey . . . well, he had never seen the likes of this before. He was off exploring.

So Whitney walked around the stomach of the fish for a while by herself. Everywhere she looked, it was the same color: a pinkish peach that had for a long time been her favorite shade. "Wow," she thought, "I wonder whether my room at home could look like this if I painted all the walls this color." After some time, however, it became too much of one shade, and she wondered when or if she'd ever see green grass again.

Needing some company, she went over to where Bailey was sniffing.

"What in Pete's name do you have in your mouth?" she said to her pup, seeing that he had found something on the floor of the stomach. It was a minnow of some sort, and it smelled awful. In fact, the whole stomach smelled like one big garbage dump.

Whitney looked over once more at Jonah and saw that he was praying. She made her way closer to him so that she could hear what he was saying:

"I called out to my Lord, and he answered me," Jonah prayed. "My Lord cast me into the deep seas, and water surrounded me, yet my God saved me. In thanksgiving, O God, I will speak to your people."

Jonah's words made Whitney very curious about what was going on between him and God. When he had finished his prayer and was resting peacefully on what felt like a soft pillow, Whitney approached Jonah. Very politely, Whitney started asking him questions.

"Jonah," she whispered modestly, "do you mind me asking you a couple of things?"

He looked into her eyes, and saw that she was sincerely curious and was determined to get the story from him. Recognizing a little bit of himself in the little girl, he smiled and shrugged, "No, go ahead."

"Well," she began, "why were you running away from God?" Of course, she was very interested in his reason because she, too, was trying to run away from going to the new school.

Jonah breathed aloud with a sigh. "That's a good question," he responded, "because now I realize that anyone in his right mind knows that you can't run away from God. However, at the time that I decided to flee, running away seemed to be my best solution.

"You see, God wanted me to go and talk to a big city of people, and tell them that if they continued to do wicked things that God would destroy their city. I really didn't want to do this for several reasons. First, I hate that city. It is called Nineveh, and it is full of mean-spirited people doing evil things. It is an awful place, and I get so angry at the people for the way they behave.

"Besides not liking the people, I figured that God would have compassion anyway. God has too much mercy to destroy the city, and I would look like a fool if, after all my attempts to make them change, they are saved. Part of me even wants the city destroyed because I think they deserve it.

"Anyway, rather than facing God, I ran away. It was the easier thing to do. It wasn't the right thing to do, but it was easier."

Jonah paused for a while, and he looked sad. "I feel like I have disappointed God, but I am going to make it up by going to Nineveh and doing what God intended me to do in the first place. My Lord has saved me from drowning in the sea, and I am thankful. I am sorry for my wrongdoing, and I don't want to run away again."

As Jonah finished his story, Whitney thought about her own situation. She realized that she, too, was trying to flee from her problem, and that she couldn't avoid the first day of school. Even if she was successful at missing the first day, she thought to herself, she wouldn't be able to run away from the school forever.

Jonah's story made sense to her. She also had wanted to do the easier thing. She was grateful that she could learn from Jonah so that she didn't have to make the same mistake.

Whitney looked around again at her surroundings. She remarked aloud, "You know, Jonah, this is how it must have been before we were born: inside our mothers' wombs. I wonder when this whale is going to give birth, if it is ever going to happen. When do you think we will see the light of day again?"

"I don't know," Jonah responded, "but I have faith in God this time. If I am to talk to the people of Nineveh, I have to get out of this fish." He thought for a second.

"Hey, do you and Bailey want to come with me to Nineveh? I would love for you to be with me there!"

"Well, I don't see why not," Whitney said, looking at Bailey, who seemed as content as could be in his new home inside the whale.

Jonah, Whitney, and Bailey spent three days and three nights inside the belly of the fish. Then God had the whale spit them out unto the dry land.

CHAPTER FOUR

NINEVEH,
WE'RE ON OUR WAY!

W hitney, Bailey, and Jonah were off to the very large city of Nineveh, the place that Jonah despised. The city was so large that if a person were to walk from one side of the city to the other, it would take him three days! The three travelers were a day's walk into the city when Whitney asked Jonah if he thought maybe it was time to start speaking aloud to the people.

"I suppose," Jonah honestly responded, "but I am still a little scared. How do I start?" he asked the little girl.

"Why don't you begin by saying exactly what the Lord ordered you to say: Repent!" Whitney directed Jonah, knowing full well that if it were she who had to do this that she wouldn't know how to begin either.

"Let's pray together for a moment. Maybe that will give you the strength to carry out God's intention," Whitney suggested.

Whitney, Jonah, and Bailey went over to a quiet, shaded area and they prayed to the Lord of Israel, the God of the heavens and the earth:

"Merciful and loving God, grant us the strength to carry out your mission. Give us the strength to speak your words to your people so that they may know of your wrath. Let them fear you as the one powerful and almighty God."

Feeling more confident, Jonah stood up from under the tree and started proclaiming to all the people within hearing distance: "Repent! I say. For the Lord of Israel will destroy your city in forty days if you do not change your sinful ways. Repent! And fear the one powerful and all-knowing Lord, the one God of heaven and of earth!"

Jonah went further into the city, and for many days and nights he pleaded with the people to repent, lest their city be destroyed. Whitney and Bailey stayed at his side as faithful and supportive friends.

"Good job, Jonah!" Whitney said, encouraging him to follow through with the mission God gave him. "God should be very pleased with you now."

News spread throughout the city of Nineveh like fire blowing through villages. Before long, everyone knew about the prophet Jonah (again, whose name meant "dove of faithfulness or truthfulness") and his message from God. Surprisingly, to Jonah, they took his words to heart. The Ninevites (the people living in Nineveh) began to fast and to wear rags for clothes.

Everywhere Jonah looked, people were changing. Where before he saw people stealing from others and doing selfish things, now he saw people being very generous, offering things to one another in kindness.

Even the king rose from his throne, took off his royal robes, and joined the others wearing rags. The king further ordered his people to fast for many days, to stop their violent and evil ways, and to cry unto God their repentance.

Making an official proclamation to the people of Nineveh, the king said:

"It is ordered today, by the decree of the king and his nobles, that every person in this city as well as every animal is to refrain from eating and drinking. No human being, no herd or flock, shall taste anything. Moreover, every person and every animal shall be covered with sackcloth. All shall turn

from their evil ways and shall cry
mightily to God.

"If we do this," the king
continued, "God may forgive us and he
may save our city."

God saw the sacrifices of Nineveh
and heard the prayers of the people
there. He knew that they had changed
their ways. And so God decided not to
destroy the city as Jonah said he would.

Jonah was disappointed by God's
mercy. He sort of expected it, which is
why he didn't want to speak to the
people in the first place. But not only
that, he really didn't like the Ninevites
and felt that they should be punished
for their wrongdoing. Jonah thought that
it wasn't fair for them to be saved after
doing a bunch of evil things for a long
time. After all, there were also very
good and faithful people who had
feared the Lord from the beginning. In

Jonah's eyes, both groups of people
were being treated the same, and that
didn't seem right.

Whitney could tell that something
was bothering Jonah, and that he was
angry. Bewildered, since his words had
been taken to heart, Whitney asked him:
"Jonah, I don't understand why
you are upset. You have been God's
messenger, and the people have heard
your words and changed their ways.
Isn't this reason for rejoicing?"
Perturbed by Whitney's goody-
goody comment, he said to his little
friend, "You don't understand. This is
why I didn't want to come in the first
place. I knew that God would be
merciful and not destroy them. The truth
is that the people of Nineveh are evil
and deserved to die. Not only does God
save them, but he makes me look like
an idiot in the process. I really don't
understand the purpose of my coming

here if God is going to change his mind anyway."

And Whitney, thinking more about what Jonah said, replied:

"But that's not the important thing here. It is because of your words, your faithful obedience to God, that the people did repent. Jonah, because you followed God's orders and warned the city, the people here have been saved."

Jonah grew even more annoyed with Whitney after she finished congratulating him. He said to her with bitterness, "This is between me and God. You and your pup should stay out of it."

Jonah went off by himself to speak alone to God.

"Lord, for this reason I ran away in the first place. I knew that you would not punish the people here because you are merciful and loving. So what was the point of my coming here?"

There was no response. Just silence. And more silence.

CHAPTER FIVE

THE MYSTERIOUS PLANT

After Jonah finished explaining his frustration to God, the angry messenger walked to the edge of the city and built himself a place to rest. He needed a break from his prophet duties and didn't feel like being with the little goody-goody, as he now saw her, and her pup.

Within the small shelter that Jonah had made for himself there suddenly grew a bush. It had miraculously sprouted and had branched off in many directions to offer Jonah great comfort, a wonderful shade over his head in the hot sun.

"Ah," said Jonah with as much relief as he had felt since God decided to save the city. "It is about time that the good people are rewarded for their efforts."

But as soon as he had said this, a small, slimy worm started attacking the bush, eating all of its branches, so that there was nothing left but withered vines. Just as the bush died, the sun rose and the wind

changed direction. Jonah became so faint that he asked God to let him die.

"Lord of Israel, God of heaven and earth, please have compassion on me. Take away my living breath and let me perish. For it is better for me to die than to live."

A little worried about Jonah, Whitney and Bailey went to look for him. There, on the eastern edge of the city, they found him underneath a small shelter. He looked extremely pale, and he was so weak that he could barely open his eyes to see who was standing beside him.

"Jonah, Jonah," Whitney whispered sweetly into his left ear. "Can you hear me, Jonah? Please talk to me. It's me, Whitney, and I have Bailey here."

Bailey jumped up onto Jonah's lap and started licking him, trying to wake him or at least get a reaction.

After five minutes of Bailey's licking him, Jonah lifted his right eyelid. He turned his head slightly.

"Who's there?" he uttered, his words barely audible, since he was extremely frail.

"It's Whitney and Bailey," she answered, overjoyed that he was finally responding to them.

He gave a half smile, and then bowed his head again.

"Jonah, we've brought you some water and a little something to eat from inside the city. If you will just lift your head slightly and open your mouth, I'll feed you."

With Whitney's diligent help, Jonah drank the water and filled his empty stomach. He was now much more awake, and began to tell Whitney what had happened with the bush.

"I'm confused," Jonah admitted to Whitney. "God gives me a beautiful bush that shaded me from the sun and then immediately destroys it. The Lord and I are obviously having a few problems communicating lately, because I really don't understand his reasoning for doing that."

Afraid to say anything that might annoy Jonah, Whitney was silent. She just listened to all what Jonah had to say, keeping her comments to herself. After he had finished his story, Whitney and Bailey decided to go play in the Tigris River and leave Jonah to himself so that he could talk to God.

Jonah then said aloud to God, "Why, Lord? Why did you create that bush for me and then have it die?"

God paused, disappointed in Jonah, and then replied:

"Don't you understand, Jonah? Don't you understand the message I was trying to tell you with the bush?"

Seeing that Jonah was confused, and obviously did not understand the point of the dying bush, God explained to him:

"Jonah, you are angry about the bush dying, yet you didn't even create or grow the bush. Still you became attached to it and were sad to see it die. Can you understand, now, why I forgave the people of Nineveh, so that they may live? I created them, and I want them to flourish in their land, as long as they stay away from wickedness. I used you to help me do this."

Jonah was silent, as he thought about what all God had said. He felt embarrassed for wanting God to destroy Nineveh because the people there had done bad things. And Jonah began to see the bigger picture, and began to understand God's great love for every creature on earth.

CHAPTER SIX

APOLOGY ACCEPTED

G od's prophet, Jonah, then went to find Whitney, who was still playing in the Tigris River with Bailey. As he came near them, he saw that they were having a grand old time. With her sandals in hand, Whitney would bend down and search the sandy shore for a large shell or small rock to toss out into the  river. Bailey would then run into the water to fetch it and bring it back to her. By the time Jonah caught up to

them, Whitney had quite a collection of beautiful shells and rocks, and Bailey looked as if he had just been through the wringer.

Feeling bad for being short-tempered with Whitney and telling her and Bailey to bug off, Jonah attempted to apologize to his dear friend.

"I am sorry, Whitney, for telling you to mind your own business. I see now that you were right—that I should be glad that God saved the city of Nineveh, and I should feel good that I was able to tell the people there to repent."

Jonah thought back to the boat, and remembered, just then, that Whitney had tried to save him from dying in the rough waters. Touched by her care for him, he became teary-eyed, and said:

"Whitney, thank you for jumping off the boat and trying to save me from drowning in the waters. I see now that you were trying to save me, just as God was trying to save his people at Nineveh."

Jonah continued, "I don't know how you got here, or what you are supposed to be doing here, but you and Bailey have helped me a great deal. You are faithful and good friends. I am so glad I had you during this difficult time."

He paused for a minute, and then asked Whitney something that had been on his mind.

"Whitney, do you ever get scared and want to run away? Have you ever wanted to hide from something, or even die in order to avoid something scary?"

Whitney smiled as she responded. "Yes, Jonah. I think that is why I am here. I am supposed to learn from you that I can't run away from my fears, and from things that I don't want to do—like go to a new school."

Jonah looked confused and asked, "What's a school?"

"It's a place where people are supposed to learn stuff together," Whitney answered. "I had been going to the same one for the last four years, and now that my family has moved, I have to start over at another one. I am scared because I don't know anyone there."

"Oh, I see." Jonah said. "Yes, I would be scared, too, like I was before talking to the people of Nineveh. But now you know that God will be with you, right?"

"Right!" Whitney exclaimed, with a new strength.

Just then, it occurred to Whitney that she might not make it to school at all the next day if she didn't get home quickly. The Emerald Bible was still bookmarked to the page where she first

started reading, before all this happened. She hoped that if she finished reading the story, as she and Nana always had, she would eventually be back home. So, before reading the last paragraph of the story, Whitney said good bye to Jonah. And Jonah, with a big hug, wished her good luck at school the next day.

Preparing herself mentally to leave the world of Jonah and to reenter her world of new friends, a new school, and all the fears that went along with both of those, Whitney began to read the last paragraph of the story:

"Then the Lord said, 'You are concerned about the bush, for which you did not labor and which you did not grow; it came into being in a night and perished in a night. And should I not be concerned about Nineveh, that great city, in which there are more than a hundred and twenty thousand persons who do not know their right hand from their left, and also many animals?'"

CHAPTER SEVEN

HURRY TO BED!

A s she suspected, as soon as Whitney finished the last word of the story, she looked up to familiar surroundings. She was, once again, seated on Nana's chair with Bailey on her lap, exactly as she had been when she first began reading.

Wiping the sweat off of her forehead, Whitney said to Bailey, "Boy, that was one good story! Wasn't it?"

Just then she heard her mother yelling from the top of the stairs, "Whitney, Whitney, you had better get to bed, Sweetheart, or else you will be exhausted for your first day of school."

"I'm coming, Mom. I'll be there in a minute," Whitney quickly replied, relieved that her mother hadn't noticed that she was gone.

Whitney looked up to heaven one last time and thanked Nana for the wonderful story, and for the wonderful lesson she had learned that evening.

ABOUT THE AUTHOR

Therese Johnson Borchard has always been inspired by the wisdom of the Bible's stories. As a young child, especially, she was intrigued by biblical characters and awed by their courage. She pursued her interest in religion and obtained a B.A. in religious studies from Saint Mary's College, Notre Dame, and an M.A. in theology from the University of Notre Dame. She has published various books and pamphlets in which she creatively retells the great stories of the Judeo-Christian tradition.

ABOUT THE ILLUSTRATOR

Wendy VanNest began drawing as a small, fidgety child seated beside her father at church. He gave her his bulletin to scribble on to help her keep still during the service. People around them began donating their bulletins, asking her for artwork, and at the end of the service, an usher would always give her his carnation boutonniere. As a result of this early encouragement, she pursued her interest and passion in art, and has been drawing ever since.